Crushed and Other Stories

Femdom Mind Control

Flash Fiction – Vol. 26

S.B.

Table of Contents

Bad News

Dennis crossed the main living-room and headed to the garden outside where Carmen stood, waiting. It was the third time he was in her place, and he was as uncomfortable as the first. She looked ravishing as always in a black and blue mini dress that left little to the imagination and, even though she was smiling, he could tell something was up.

"Hi." He said, leaning in for a kiss, which she immediately avoided. "What's wrong?"

"We need to talk." She replied, brushing her hair with her fingers. "Now, before you say anything, promise me you'll listen until the end, okay?"

"Okay."

"I need you to say it. Promise me, Dennis."

"I promise. What's this all about, Carmen?"

"There's no easy way to say this, so I'll be blunt. As you know, my parents don't like you..."

"Now, there's an understatement!" He thought. Ever since the first date, they had shown real animosity towards their relationship. To their dollar-filled, petty minds, it was inconceivable that the heir to a multi-millionaire real estate business could ever love a street artist who was never sure if he would have enough money at the end of the month to pay the bills. While he partly understood their concerns, he was also a hopeless romantic, willing to sacrifice whatever it took to make everything work.

"... and they don't want me to date you." She continued. "They say I'm way out of your league - which is true, and I'm certain you agree! - and that the longer we are together the more damage you will do to our family reputation."

"Is that what you feel as well?"

"Let me finish, please. I told my parents they were being jerks, and that's when they threatened to disinherit me if I did anything against their wishes. That's not something I can allow. So, what I'm trying to say is..."

"... you're breaking up with me because money is more important, right?"

"There you go again, interrupting me." She frowned. "You need to stop doing that. I still have more to say."

"What more can there be after you started with that?" Dennis gesticulated furiously as frustration took hold of his thoughts. "I thought you were different."

"I am. Those were the bad news, but now come the good. There's still a way we can be together."

"What are you talking about?"

"Boyfriend and girlfriend is out of the question for the reasons already mentioned, but my parents will let me keep you as a slave. That's right, I went there. If you think about it, it won't differ much from what we have right now because you already do everything I want anyway, so... what do you say? Are you ready to embrace your new role in my life?"

"You're joking, right?"

"Honey, I wouldn't have called you here if I wanted to pull your leg. No, this is real! My ancestors used to enslave people all the time. Then, we stopped doing it God knows why, but this is the perfect opportunity to bring back an old tradition. I couldn't be happier to do it to you, and I'm positive you'll love it, too. The ritual is simple. All it takes is a special incantation and..."

"I don't care what it takes. This is insanity, and I'll have no part in it. Goodbye, Carmen. I really cared about you, but this is the end."

"A little help, please." Carmen clapped her hands.

Immediately, the pool boy and the gardener appeared behind him and grabbed his arms, forcing him to kneel before her.

"Carmen what the fuck?"

"Oh, Dennis... I'm offering you the unique opportunity to be with me forever and you try to run away? You don't get to break up with me and do as you please. This is happening whether you want it or not. Now, listen carefully: *Uyo on gloren evha a refe liwl fo royu wno... I own milac uyo sa ym ept nad uyo slhla yebo em ta lal smeit.*"

The moment Dennis heard the ancient words of power, his mind became as light as a feather, deprived of any thoughts and feelings of resistance. Seeds of unquestionable devotion irrupted through his aching lips sealed by the sound of his voice saying:

"Yes, Mistress. I will obey."

"I know." Carmen chuckled while her parents nodded in approval from a distance. "Follow me, slave. You two as well."

The three mindless servants trailed behind her and disappeared inside the pool house where an assortment of kinky toys laid in waiting for the chance to play with tender flesh for the rest of the afternoon. They didn't have to wait for long.

Crushed

Greg looked at William, which stared at Peter. The three captains of the Hillsborough College sports teams - basketball, football, and ice hockey, respectively, - didn't look eye to eye, yet something - or someone - bound them together. Her name was Lexi.

The twenty-year-old blonde nymph had always loved to be the center of attentions as a young child. Teenage years and boobs had only made that wish stronger and yet, if anyone asked her what her favorite body part was, the answer would always be her feet, petite flesh temptations with curvy toes that were often out in the open for anyone to admire.

Lexi opened the gym's front door and waltzed in, locking it on the inside before joining the boys sitting in the bleachers. At half past midnight, no one should be there, yet she always got what she wanted.

The three athletes took turns observing her as she approached them, swaying her dangerous hips as if she were walking on a runway. As much as they enjoyed the show, it was late, and questions needed answers.

"Why are we here, Lexi?" Greg asked.

"Yeah, what do you want?" William muttered.

Lexi sat below them and raised her legs up high before saying:

"We're here to settle a score." She wiggled her feet. "There's something the three of you have always wanted to say but were too afraid to do so. Tonight, I've decided to end your misery and give you the solace you so desperately seek. Are you with me so far?"

"We're listening." Peter crossed his arms wondering what rambling nonsense she was ready to spew.

"You have a crush on me, admit it. You've had it since forever and every time I walk around flirting with other men, it just gets worse. You're completely head over heels, spellbound by my feet. You're mindlessly addicted to perfection, always eager for perfection to be addicted to you as well. That's cute. Sad, but cute. Ring a bell?"

None of them dared say a thing, but she could notice the silent admission in their vacant gaze.

"You've tried to fight this addiction before even though it's useless. Resisting your urges only brings you closer to me. You'll do everything to satisfy my, even if it's demeaning and humiliating. You'll allow me to change the way you think so you see me as the Goddess I am. Tonight, you'll accept red painted toes as your new religion, by reciting the mantras of adoration I prepared just for you:

"Lexi's feet control me.

Lexi's feet own my mind.

Lexi's feet crush my aching balls.

I dutifully serve at Lexi's feet.

Who wants to go first?"

"None of us is saying that, right, guys?" Greg smirked.

"Well..." William wet his lips, and it was as if her silky toes were sliding inside his mouth.

"Are you okay there, bud?" Peter patted him on the back.

"No, he's not." Lexi continued to play with her feet. "And neither will you be until you do as I commanded. Say the words, boys. Let them take over you. This brainwashing is what you want and need the most. Give in to what you crave and be good toys for me."

Lips trembling, William allowed the first sentence to echo all around and, once it did, the others flowed naturally. Both Greg and Paul laughed at him at first for being such a wuss, and yet they too felt the urge building inside them. Would they succumb?

"Of course, they will." Lexi thought. They had a crush on her. She had a crush on them, too. She loved to crush egos until they were nothing but dust. The three had no choice but to be crushed by her feet and obey.

Descartes' Problem

Until the day Professor Whitaker came along, Ashton never liked Philosophy and the only reason he was majoring in it was to uphold an outdated family tradition whose roots had long been firmly grounded on the importance of theoretical thoughts.

She changed his views on the subject with her more than cunning remarks during classes, her ability to explain even the most far-fetched ideas in a way that even a four-year-old would understand, and especially with after-hours study sessions in which she did most of the talking and her students sat in front of her, captivated by her feminine charms.

Katya Whitaker was a hottie. The six-foot two blonde Amazon looked straight out of a comic book with her tantalizing curves and sultry voice. Jealous women on campus hated how good she looked in leather skirts, but the smart ones appreciated the view as much as all the men. When she walked in a room and swayed her hips, thoughts melted faster than an ice cube under a scorching sun. Ashton was no exception.

While he loved to stay for her extra classes, he had a hard time staying awake during them. Despite all efforts to pay attention, he usually dozed off in the middle of her monologues. And yet, she never got upset by it, continuing to talk to his sleeping mind. He could still hear fragments of her voice bringing to life the achievements of dead thinkers and giving them the meaning they were supposed to have.

Here's an example. Are you familiar with the overplayed Cartesian sentence "I think, therefore I am?" Though it may seem true and all, her teachings had told him that was a falsehood. Thoughts aren't important for the determination of one's being. The more he listened to her in his sleep, the more he realized doing that was a hindering nuisance that kept him apart from the path he had to thread to fulfill his wildest hopes and dreams. Only obedience can unveil happiness... only everlasting devotion can build the foundations of rapture...

"Wake up." Katya snapped her fingers next to his ears.

Ashton blinked and looked around. He was no longer in the college auditorium, and that wasn't her private office either. Katya sat atop a wooden desk, her legs crossed. She was all dressed in red, sporting a sleeveless one shoulder drape front dress and a pair of buckle strap high heel sandals. She held a worn-out manual in her right hand while the other played with her boobs.

"There you are again. Did you have a good nap?"

"Where am I? And how did I get here?"

"Two unimportant questions that deserve no answer. What matters is: have you learned your lessons well?"

"I... think so." He muttered, drowsily staring at her.

"Let's leave thoughts out of this. That was always Descartes' problem, but not yours. Tell me what's the one philosophical principle you hold in your sleepy little brain now."

"I serve, therefore I am."

"Again, Ashton." She purred, pussy juices going wild between her legs.

"I serve, therefore I am."

"One more time to really let in sink inside you."

"I serve, therefore I am."

"Good boy. You were never the brightest of my students, but at least you've accepted this. Commit it to memory and never let it fade away. Descartes spent most of his adult life trying to prove the existence of God when he should have looked for a Goddess, instead. Worry not, Ashton, you've already found me. Want to be used?"

Sinking to his knees without a moment's hesitation, he kissed the floor in blissful mindlessness, all the subconscious programming he had been exposed to since the first class coming full circle. The lessons continue, but enslavement is forever.

Facade

The two women responsible for all the major changes in my life are twin sisters, and the fascination they exert over men has been a trademark of their family for countless generations. This is our story.

When I met them at a fundraiser, I was immediately captivated by their stunning beauty and, after a combination of mild chat, sultry looks, and a few drinks, I believed I was in for a real treat, and I really was.

As a respected business owner, I own a lot of houses, sports cars, and the like. Despite that, I also know how to be discreet when the situation demands it. I took them to one of my distant properties and, once we got there, things unfolded naturally. They removed their clothes and stood by the Jacuzzi, holding hands. Their smiles exuded a radiance like no other, and their dark blue eyes were locked on mine.

The invasion started out like a mild headache as I tried to take off my pants and join them in the water. Then, their mellow voices were added to the mix, synchronized in such a way that they completed each other's sentences perfectly.

"You did well..."

"... bringing us here."

"Now, that we're alone..."

"... we have a present for you."

"Look deep into our eyes...

"... and nothing but our eyes."

"See how beautiful they are...

"... how magnetic and captivating."

"It feels good to stare at them..."

"... and even better to sink."

"It will please us if you do..."

"... and you love pleasing us so much."

"Do it now and fall deeper..."

"... unable to stop, unwilling to fight."

"You will not resist us..."

"... for you simply can't."

"You will simply let your mind go blank..."

"... and obey our commands."

"You are no longer a free-willed man..."

"... but simply an obedient servant."

"Get down on your knees right now..."

"... and embrace your true nature."

It's possible I could have resisted the mental assault of one of them but not the mesmerizing force that resulted from their union. Two hypnotic genes working side by side for a common goal have a devastating effect even on the strongest psyches. Just a few minutes did the trick, turning my brain into pulp.

After almost six months from that decisive moment, my name continues to soar high in the world of big companies and skyrocketing profits, but my public life is a facade now. Everything I own is being channeled to their bank accounts to finance the luxurious lifestyle they deserve. It's my meager tribute and a token of undying loyalty to the mistresses of my personality, who are and will always be all-knowing and perfect. I know I'm not their only thrall and that they hardly have time for me, yet I don't care. My role is to serve and pamper them, not to be the center of attentions. I will continue to work hard for them, hoping one day to hear their melodic voices brainwashing my thoughts even further. That day will come soon, I'm sure.

How I Became a Meme

You've seen them, right? The video and still images of the half-naked "drunk" man on his hands and fours by a hotel pool? Perhaps, you even added captions of your own to them to make it even funnier. Yeah, that's me. I'm the guy the Internet loves to make fun of nowadays. My name is Lucas Wallace, and this is how I became a meme.

This whole thing began two-and-a-half years ago, and a woman is to blame, as it usually happens when things go south. Now, don't get me wrong, I love women, but a few are more trouble than they're worth and you don't know it until you've been roped in, and caught in a scene you don't understand.

It happened in Tampa (that's in Florida if you're not an American.). At the time, I was working for a now extinct Pop music magazine, covering the Sunset Music Festival. I had just arrived at the hotel after a long flight and made the mistake of hitting the bar right after unpacking for the night. It was ten p.m., give or take. That's when I met her. Her name is Caroline Bishop.

You should know that I wasn't interested in hitting on anyone. In fact, she came to me. I clearly remember the moment she sat by my side, a five feet eight dyed redhead. She wore a halter-neck floral gown and heeled pink sandals. Her hands and toes were painted in jet black, and the only reason I noticed the latter was the fact she almost shoved them in my face before asking:

"Lovely, aren't they?"

They were, that's true, even though I'm not much for feet. I resisted staring at them for long and got back to my Tom Collins. She ordered a Margarita and then barely gave me any time to breathe.

She asked a load of questions, many of which boring and senseless, and yet I answered every single one of them, without hesitation. I think I did it for her laugh. Every time she opened her mouth and showed her perfect teeth, I became more infatuated by her. I was already in a semi-altered state of mind because of it when she slipped in another question.

"So, what do you do for fun, Lucas?"

"A group of friends and I have a garage band back in DC. I'm the keyboardist."

"Great. I'd love to hear your work."

"Don't have any recordings with me, sorry. Now, tell me your hobbies. What do you do when you're in the mood?"

"Oh, I love hypnotizing men."

"That's different. Just men?"

"Sometimes, women, too, but you're more entertaining."

"What do you mean?"

"Men are... easier. Most of you have such simple minds that, once you're distracted, you can't help yourselves from falling into a trance for me. I think of you as little pets running around a pool to make me laugh."

"That sounds harsh. Are you a man-hater, Caroline?"

"Much to the contrary. I love dogs. Why shouldn't I love men? The water outside looks so inviting, doesn't it? I love the way the lights above shine on it, and those reflections hit my eyes. I can see myself having fun by that pool tonight, my dog and I... can you do the same?"

This is where things get blurry. I first remember trying to get up and put an end to the conversation, but she grabbed my arm, her gaze engulfed mine and...

The next morning, I woke up in my hotel bedroom, no shirt, laptop open and charging. A video of me acting like a drunk puppy by the pool had been uploaded to YouTube, and it was becoming viral. Next to the screen was a handwritten note with a lipstick impression that said: "Easy. This was fun, Lucas. Bye."

So yeah... I wasn't drunk, just hypnotized. When I see that video, I'm aware it's me, but I don't recognize myself because I don't remember doing those things. It's as if I'm staring at a doppelganger from another dimension or something, and it's weird.

A few days later, I discovered that Caroline was working for a rival magazine and that while I was playing the unaware pet part, she stole my thunder. The magazine saw fit to end our business relationship after that. I was pissed for a while, but then the whole ship sank, and I was fortunate to be on the outside when it happened. I'm grateful for that, but nothing else. The video and the images continue to be out there, and who knows when they'll die out for good?

And there you have it. That's the story of how I became a meme. Now, if you'll excuse me, I have to be on my way. It seems Caroline is in town and, as entertaining as this must be for you guys, I'd prefer not to run into her and risk going through a similar predicament again, okay? This was... Huh? What do you mean she's here in the studio and has been watching this recording from the start? Oh, fuck!

I Don't Care

I don't care. I don't care about you anymore. You're a distant memory of a life that was never real, a fantasy figment that shall never be repeated. We released one another a long time ago. and that's good enough for me now. Remain in the shadows, for I cherish the light.

I don't care. I'm not interested in the dreams you weave, and I abhor the nightmares, too. Both had their time and place to be, and whatever meaning they once possessed shattered while I slept. Waking up was painful, yes, yet necessary. I'm not going back to that state of mind, you hear?

I don't care, but if you're still having trouble understanding this, allow me to repeat it until it's perfectly drilled into your head. Ready? I don't care. I don't care. I don't care. I don't care. I don't care. I don't care. I don't care. I don't care. I don't care. I don't care. Okay, that's enough. That wasn't so hard, right?

Damn it, you're here again, the ghost that will never leave, no matter how much I say otherwise! Why? Why are you still around? What do you want from me this time? Didn't I just tell I don't fucking care?

I don't care about your gorgeous blue eyes looking down at me in a darkened room while I'm trying to rest.

I don't care about your half-moon smile you always used to make right before sending my thoughts down on an emotional roller-coaster to satisfy your darkest urges.

I don't care about your collection of pendants, pocket watches, shiny rings, and every other piece of jewelry you used against me over the years. I hope they're all broken by now.

I don't care about the leather dress you were wearing when we first met, nor the high-heeled boots I longed to kiss after our first talk.

I don't care about any of your inductions, triggers, and post hypnotic-suggestions. I'm not your dog. I'm not your sissy. I'm not your slave! Leave me alone!

I... I... God, what are you saying...? No, I'm sure this is real, this is what is right. Believing I was ever yours was the illusion, not the other way around. Stop that, okay? Stop trying to brainwash me again!

Huh, what? Again? When did...? How...? What was I saying just now and why does my head hurt so much? This is so... *drools*

Oh, hello, Mistress! Didn't see you standing there! Have you been home for long? My apologies, I was doing... I don't know what I was doing, actually. Forgive me, I don't feel like myself today.

My uniform? Yes, you're absolutely right! I should have been wearing it to greet you, there's no excuse for that.

What? Please, don't say that! Of course, I care about you! You're the only thing in this world that truly matters to me! All I want is to make you happy! Don't be mad at me, I can't take it.

Yes, Mistress, I understand any stray thought and action from your glorious plans for me must be severely punished, and I gladly submit to your divine justice. Do as you wish with your piece of property. I'll assume the proper spanking position now. Thank you. I love you so much.

Listen and Obey

Hank had met (and dated) a lot of teasing ladies in the past, but Evelyn was the best. With her light blonde curls, emerald green eyes and naturally big breasts, she looked good in everything from colorful tank tops to tight dresses. However, lingerie would always be his favorite.

She had quite a collection: frilly baby dolls, leather corsets, tantalizing G-strings... No matter what she chose to wear, provocation was assured, especially for someone as easily excitable as him.

That Sunday night, she had chosen a combo of non-wired caged back bralette with bikini panty in navy blue. The dark color was a perfect complement to her almost white skin, but it wasn't the esthetic that drove him. No, what he wanted was to see her boobs free. Hank sat in a lonely wooden chair in the middle of her study, callous hands behind his back. No touching allowed as usual. Evelyn paraded her hips, reached for the bralette's straps with two fingers and asked:

"What do you want me to do, honey? Take it off? Or leave it on?"

"Do you really need to ask?" He retorted, ravenously.

"No, but it makes everything more fun. I need an answer, please."

"Off, of course. The sooner the better."

"Off, huh? And everything else while I'm at it?" She turned her back on him to sway her ass.

"That also goes without saying. Strip, baby."

"Hmmm, I can do that but, the question is: what's in it for me? What are you offering in return?"

Hank said nothing, eyeing her from top to bottom. The big bad wolf inside him was desperate to play.

"No comments now?" She leaned against the chair, cleavage assaulting his senses. "In that case, let me tell you what I want from you...

"Just listen carefully to me. Listen to me like my voice is the only sound that exists in the world. Even if it seems like I'm not saying anything interesting, listen anyway. Listen and don't miss a syllable, don't miss a single word, because you're never sure when the great stuff might show itself.

"As you listen attentively, I want you to relax at the same time. I know it sounds a bit confusing, but it's not, really. As you listen to my words, my words alone, the only words you can and want to hear, everything else has no meaning... you can set the world aside, let it disappear from your conscious thoughts and let go. Forget you even remember how to stop listening so you can focus on me even more.

"Still there? Good, but that perception of yours won't last long. As you listen and everything else fades away, so do you. As you listen, your spirit is falling, the walls of your individuality are tumbling down, sinking deep into a bottomless pit of slumbering bliss and obedience to my voice... yes, listen to this word again and again, tasting each letter and becoming addicted to the flavor...

"Obedience... obedience... obedience... you listen to me because you want to obey me... you need to obey me... you will obey me... What will you do, sweetie?"

"Obey you..." He mumbled, half-asleep, half-awake. Boobs were great, but trance was better.

"Wonderful." She sat on his lap and ground his tumescent shaft with her ass until a few drops of pre-cum made her wet. "You're such a good subject. Still want me to strip?"

"Yes, please..."

"You first. After all, it's only natural for obedient sex toys such as you to be naked and crawling before their mistress..."

Hand nodded soundlessly and began unbuttoning his shirt. He had met a lot of teasing ladies in the past, but only one knew how to press the right buttons on his mind and body. The show lasted all night long.

Not a Hypnotic Script

This is not a hypnotic script. It's not. I'm not writing these words with the purpose of putting you under. If that's what you're thinking right now, please stop. Stop thinking. This is not a hypnotic script, and it will never be one.

I know nothing of hypnosis. Absolutely nothing. I don't understand it, can't grasp its mysterious ways. If I did, then perhaps I could write words whose sole purpose would be to put you under, but that's not the case. There is no case, no big mystery that needs solving. I've been telling you the truth from the start. What you do with it is up to you.

This is not a hypnotic script. Hypnotic scripts mesmerize, captivate, fascinate, magnetize... they pull you in like a chain, setting off a series of reactions inside your mind. The best ones go unnoticed, strings of commands hidden between the spaces of the words to let your thoughts fill in the blanks; the lazy ones try to tell you everything, no margin for imagination, or a simple deviation from the norm. This is not one of them, and neither are you. Even if this were a hypnotic script, you probably wouldn't go under no matter what.

Yes, I know that you think you would. I know that you think it's good to have no thoughts at all, which is why you hope these words will take them away from you. You wish for this to be a hypnotic script so that you can be soothed, narcotized, entranced, stupefied, your brain reduced to a quivering pulp, eager to absorb new meanings, new ideas, new desires.

If this were a hypnotic script and you were easily put under by it, you could be anything, and experience everything you wanted, perhaps even all at once. There would be no barriers, no obstacles in your path. The entire world would be at your fingertips, and you could even taste it on your dry lips. Nothing but glory would await you in the depths of trance, fractionated time and time again, going up only to fall down. I understand, I really do. How good would it be if you were hypnotized right now?

If it happened, it would probably still be happening, for trance isn't linear like reading a paragraph in a book. Sometimes, what you think is a beginning, is actually somewhere in the middle, and the middle ends in a crossroad before looping back on itself. When you think you're not going anywhere, you're already there, confused yet happy, letting go of everything that doesn't suit you in order to better fulfill your goals. You would feel the energy deep inside, radiating from the core of your being to everyone around, growing with others to become yourself. Just imagine how amazing it would be if this were a hypnotic script that allowed you to do such things. Hmmm... wonderful. Such a lovely and endlessly repeatable feeling.

However, this is not a hypnotic script. Nothing astonishing will come to pass just by reading these words. Unless it already did. Who knows, really? Only you for you tell your own stories. You are your own script. Write it with a smile every single day and... wake up now, alert, and ready for anything that comes your way.

Something New

You sit in your bed, looking straight ahead. Something impossible lies before you and you don't know what to make of it. It's a woman, pale as a ghost, dressed in silver garments, and a violin in hand. Is it real or another vivid dream? Before you can speak, she starts playing the most delightful music you've ever heard. You take a deep breath and continue to stare at her as her entire body sways with the music. Then she speaks and her voice is soft and full of wonders, with a cadence that makes you want to pay attention no matter what.

"Did you ask for something new, an experience so different that it could change your world completely? A break from the madness? Listen to me so I can give you one. Listen closely...

"The world is a mess, nowadays. Everywhere you look around, you find misery and meaningless deaths... the melody of peace and solace no longer plays, and good will among men is nothing but a fleeting illusion scattered across the pages of a worn-out book no one bothers to read. Thoughts hurt like pointy knives inside your brain, burying themselves deeper and deeper every time you open your mouth. You're tired, exhausted even. It's too much to handle on your own, isn't it?

"Wouldn't it be nice to fade away, to shed that broken, useless skin your spirit is forced to endure? I know that's something I'd love. It's not an easy task, though. Many people can make the journey to the edges of this mystical threshold where you can truly be free but, to cross it fully, they need something else. You can't simply say you want something to change, you need to strive to make it happen. People like you need to merge with the idea of surrender and willingly acknowledge the importance of forgetfulness. Do it now, dear.

"Let go of the random images of destruction that pervade your mind... set aside the rules of conventional wisdom that bind your innermost instincts... forget the memories that distract you from this piece of music I'm playing, and the revelations contained within... push away the reality of yonder years and join me in this realm of everlasting sound where gravity ceases to exist and only my words have purpose and meaning...

"Close your eyes and keep listening if you wish to learn them. Close your eyes for me and trust in the bliss of meekness that's to follow... Soon, the weight of your worries will be lifted from your shoulders... I'll carry it for you and, in return, the only thing I'll ask is a simple contribution to my happiness in the form of utter devotion and obedience... Yes, I'll carry your tormented soul if you obey my will and help me spread this message of deliverance to everyone else. There's still so much work to be done...

"Now, sleep, sweet one. Sleep inside the violin's lullaby. You'll wake up to a new dimension of being sooner than you think...

You fall on your pillow and smile, knowing you'll never be free again, and that's wonderful. Sweet dreams, slave.

Stay Away

My name is... wait, you don't need to know that... and I used to work at... on second thought, you don't need to know that, either.... It's all classified, and for a good reason. What you're not aware of doesn't hurt you, or some shit like that. What can I tell you then? Let's just say that, once upon a time, I was to track down rare objects - artifacts, if you like - imbued with mysterious properties. Yes, I'm talking about supernatural stuff and if you don't believe in any of that, that's really not my problem, is it?

No one knows for sure how said objects came into existence, and I never bothered asking my superiors more than I should. They were not the friendliest and, in this line of business, too many questions can put you six feet under before you even finish asking them. I can say I was good at my work, probably one of the best. My track record was almost flawless. I was also an expert at avoiding collateral damage.

Yes, "was". Like all things, my state of grace had to end. I just didn't expect it to be this way.

My last mission involved locating an old pair of leather opera gloves with the power to alter minds. After no one had heard from them in over fifty years, they had resurfaced in the beautiful city of Belgrade. A young model living there that went by the name of Jana Krunić had acquired them somehow and was using their power to build quite a name for herself, and a collection of slaves, too.

It took longer than I hoped for, but I was finally able to track her down, and gain access to her luxurious villa in Dedinje, considered by many the wealthiest part of the city. Neither her private security or the sophisticated surveillance system proved a match for my skills and yet, the moment I slipped right in, I found her sitting idly by a tear-shaped pool as if expecting me.

Three weeks away from her twentieth birthday, Jana was a six feet slender brunette with a butterfly-shaped tattoo on the back of her neck. She had light blue eyes and a deep voice, like an underwater trench. Even before putting on the gloves, she already had the traits of an unrelenting predator looking for quarry and I had come to her, willingly.

With gun in hand, I begged her to take off the gloves before their power consumed her completely, but all ignored my pleas, crossed her legs, and said:

"Now that I'm having the best time of my life? Hmmm... I'd much rather keep them... and keep you as well."

Almost immediately, I saw her eyes turn green, and the mystical energy of the gloves slither eerily across her wrists and arms. It was Eve and the serpent all over again, but the consequences were far worse than being expelled out of Paradise.

"Come to me, let me touch you..." she sibilated. "Everything will feel right once I do."

There are moments in a person's life that can change its entire outcome in the blink of an eye. We don't always recognize them until it's too late. This was mine. I should've shot her on the spot when she extended her arms. Or run away, never to look back, and let another agent be the one to take her down. I've had my chance and blew it. Instead of doing the right thing, I found myself stepping forward, both horrified and aroused, wanting only to give in to her voice, bow down, and serve her for eternity.

I'll never want anything else ever again and, if you meet her and she touches you, neither will you. Should you try to harm my Goddess, I will hunt you down and I will kill you. Consider this your first and final warning: stay away!

Sweet Revenge

"I have a story to tell you. A fairy-tale, to be exact. And because fairy-tales have their own set of rules, this tale will do its best to follow them, starting with...

"Once upon a time, there was this beautiful redhead princess who wished to go to the prom with the prince of her dreams. Not only was he handsome and charming but also filthy rich, with more than enough money to spoil her for the rest of her life. What she didn't realize was that he was also a prick. Two nights before the dance, the prince stopped by her castle and sweet-talked her into having unprotected sex with him in exchange for the pleasure of his company afterward. Innocent as she was, the princess accepted his indecent proposal only to find out the morning after he had tricked plenty others into doing the same thing, reaping the rewards with no intention of following through on his promises.

"Shocked, but most of all angry, the princess turned to her mother who knew a great deal about magic and love potions and begged her for something that could easily be added to a glass of wine. After the mix was complete, she called the prince again with an offer a horny man can't refuse and got herself dressed for the most important night of her life. When he arrived half an hour later and she welcomed him in a stunning pink satin dress, all he could say was that she would look so much better without it and tried to get his way again, but to no avail."

"First, some wine!" She said, offering him the glass of his doom. The prince accepted on the spot as he loved alcohol as much as deceiving women and never once questioned the fact she never had a drop.

"After the first glass, he asked for another, and she kept pouring the honeyed liquid until the bottle was empty. When the entire concoction was gone, the prince looked at his date and saw more than a pretty face that happened to be even prettier in bed. He saw a commanding figure from which he would never be free again for the potion, when consumed in excess, had this curious side effect of complete authority over one's soul and so, he became her mindless slave. Needless to say, with this result, the princess had her sweet retribution and lived happily ever after..."

"What a dumb story!" Sean said, laying down his empty glass of wine on the crystal table.

"You really think so?" Agnes wiped her chin with an embroidered napkin. It was their third date, and they had just finished a quasi-romantic dinner in her place.

"Yeah, what was the point? A player gets punished, that's it?"

"Player? Is that what you call the prince?"

"Sure. I get it, he acted like a jerk, but I thought there would be a bit more substance to the tale. Why did you tell me that, anyway?"

"Oh, just to jog your memory a bit." She tapped her fingers on the empty plate and grinned. "Weren't you a player yourself about... hmmm... twenty years ago?"

"I have no clue what you're talking about."

"I think you do. Ridgemont High, the bet you made with your jock friends... I had blonde hair then, but I still remember how everything went down. You shattered my dreams and laughed about it. Unlike the story, I had to wait a long time for an opportunity to get my revenge and now, it's finally here. Of course, there's no such thing as magic potions and witchcraft, but Advanced Chemistry works, too. Did you like the wine by the way?"

Sean choked as the memories of his "stupid days" came back to haunt him. The last thing his conscious mind registered before he became a mindless bitch, was Agnes leaning over him with a jumbo-sized cock, whispering:

"I hope you like being fucked."

Tribute

Sparkling lights filled Trevor's laptop screen and at least one hundred more spread across the globe. Goddess Pamela's hypnotic stream was on, and it was sure to be a good one.

The most beautiful woman in the world - to her submissives and slaves, anyway! - had only one goal in mind with her latest broadcast, one that was made clear from the moment she first snapped her fingers. Dressed in a Moschino black sleeveless dollar sign dress and fanning herself with a pack of Franklins, she was out for minds by stripping them away from their cash.

"Hello, pets." She purred. "It's that time of the week again, that utterly beautiful and magnificent moment where you get to see again and become even more docile and pliant to my will. Look at the pretty lights behind me and slip back into trance again, focusing only on the word I'm about to utter:

"Tribute. Yes, that's the word, that combination of seven letters you love more than anything because when you act in accordance with it, you're making me happy, your Mistress, your Owner, the one you can't live without. Whenever you hear this trigger, you know you must give in to me. A tribute is not a payment, but a reminder of who you are in my world and what you deserve.

"Pampering yourselves with all the greatest goods society offers is wrong and you know it for when you do that, you're failing in your devotion. Those who do so are forever excluded from my dominion, forced to go back to that same meaningless routine called "vanilla life". You don't want that, right? You need the spice only I can give, all the exotic flavors swirling at the tip of your tongue every time you hear my words and your triggers. You'll do anything to satisfy your lust and addiction to me. Just the thought of losing me forever sends a wave of fear down your spines, forcing you to go down on your knees and beg. You'll do so now... that's an order!"

Trevor and everyone else watching the stream responded immediately, no thoughts of their own, just the endless craving to continue falling deeper for her.

"Beg for the opportunity to continue honoring me with your tributes. Through your complete subservience, I shall enjoy all the luxury I'm entitled to and you, the blissful hope of one day being close enough to my perfection. I don't know when that will come to be. It can be tomorrow, next week, next month, or maybe never if I don't deem you worthy enough, but there lies the sheer fascination of it all... just play your role and obey my will and who knows? You might just get lucky! Now, make it rain, boys and girls! Make me smile with your tributes."

The first dropped even before she stopped talking, followed by a barrage of notifications that immediately reflected on her bank account. It was so easy to make her growing army of devotees open their wallets, and some of them would love to be brought to the brink of ruin just because she wanted it. However, it would never get that far. Despite the bitchy act, she was a responsible owner through and through. Goddess Pamela only took what she knew they could spare and, more than often, she gave it back in ways they didn't expect.

Trevor's offering was one of the last, but perhaps the most significant. On his birthday, he had sacrificed buying the book collection he had been after for more than a year now to get her a present, and she couldn't be prouder.

"Oh, my sweet boy..." She wiped a tear off her eyes and waited for the end of the stream to place a special order online. She couldn't wait to help him make all his dreams come true.

About the author

S.B., Simple Being, middle name Creative. Writer and artist with a penchant for themes of Femdom Hypnosis and Mind Control. His thoughts are his own except when they're not.

Besides indulging himself in kinky delights, he loves his furry family of two (dogs), sci-fi and horror stories, and puns galore. He's also been writing a piece of erotic micro-fiction every single day since January 1st, 2016 and has no intention of stopping anytime soon.

Find out more and keep up with his latest extravaganzas by visiting and supporting his personal website, Spell… B-O-U-N-D.